My Baby Brother IS a Little Monster

By Sarah Albee
Illustrated by Tom Brannon

Dalmatian Press, LLC, 2007. All rights reserved.
Published by Dalmatian Press, LLC, 2007. The DALMATIAN PRESS name and logo are trademarks of Dalmatian Press, LLC, Franklin, Tennessee 37067. No part of this book may be reproduced or copied in any form without written permission from the copyright owner.

Printed in the U.S.A.
ISBN: 1-40373-213-2 (X)

07 08 09 BM 10 9 8 7 6 5 4 3 2 1
15689 Sesame Street 8x8 Storybook: My Baby Brother is a Little Monster

"Hi, Henry," said Big Bird. "Ready to go to the park?"

"I'm ready," replied Henry. "But my mom can't take us until my brother wakes up from his nap."

"Oh, okay," said Big Bird.

Henry sighed. "We have to play inside until he's ready."

"Nice to see you, Big Bird," said Henry's mother.
"Calvin should be awake soon."

Just then, Big Bird heard a horrible noise. "Wow!
What's that?" he said.

Henry rolled his eyes. "That's my brother.
He's awake."

"Big Bird," said Henry, "meet Calvin."
Big Bird smiled at Calvin.
Calvin drooled and blew bubbles.

"Can we go to the park now?" Henry asked.
"In a few minutes," said Henry's mother.

"Mom, come see the cool castle we made," Henry called.
Just at that moment, Calvin dumped a box of cereal all over the floor.

While his mother was cleaning up the cereal, Calvin crawled over and knocked down the castle.

"Gee," said Big Bird. "You want to play jacks or something?"

Henry shook his head sadly. "Nah, we can't. Calvin might try to put them in his mouth. You're not supposed to play with little toys when there's a baby around."

"Mom, *now* can we go to the park?" asked Henry.

"Pretty soon, honey," replied his mother. "Oh, isn't your brother adorable? Let me take a picture of the two of you together."

"Ouch!" said Henry.

"Why don't you tell him not to do that?" asked Big Bird.

"He doesn't understand that it hurts," replied Henry.

"He's just a *little* monster."

"*Eeeew*! Mom!" called Henry, holding his nose. "Calvin needs to be changed!"

Henry's mother carried Calvin away to change his diaper.

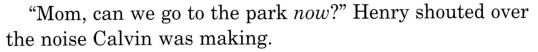

"Mom, can we go to the park *now*?" Henry shouted over the noise Calvin was making.

"Soon, honey," his mother shouted back. "Calvin's hungry. I have to feed him. Then can we go."

"Your baby brother sure is loud!" yelled Big Bird.

"I wish you'd hurry up and eat that!" Henry told his brother.
SPLAT! Calvin decided he was finished with his lunch.
"Wow," said Big Bird. "Your baby brother sure is messy."

Henry had had enough. "I'm sick of having a baby around! He makes dumb baby noises and he messes up my toys and he throws food around. I wish," said Henry, his lip starting to tremble, "I wish I didn't have a baby brother!"

Henry's mother gave Henry a big hug. "Sweetie, I know it can be hard to have a little brother. It's okay to feel angry with him sometimes. Calvin is lucky to have such a patient big brother."

"Really?" said Henry, wiping his eyes.

"Come on! Let's go to the park!" said his mother.

A little while later, as they were playing catch, Big Bird stopped. "Hey, Henry," he said softly, "I think Calvin just said your name."

Henry hurried over to Calvin. "Mom!" he shrieked. "Hey, Mom! Calvin said my name!"

Henry's mother ran over to listen, too.

"En-wee, En-wee," Calvin said.